Isla saw the wolves' muscles bunch. They were about to spring! She tensed, and then, suddenly, a little unicorn came bursting out of the nearby trees and charged at the wolves.

"Buttercup!" Isla shrieked, her head spinning. What was her unicorn doing there?

LOOK OUT FOR MORE ADVENTURES AT

UNICORN ACADEMY

Sophia and Rainbow

Scarlett and Blaze

Ava and Star

Isabel and Cloud

Layla and Dancer

Olivia and Snowflake

Rosa and Crystal

Ariana and Whisper

Matilda and Pearl

Freya and Honey

Violet and Twinkle

Isla and Buttercup

★ ★ ★

UNICORN ✷ ACADEMY ✷
Isla and Buttercup

WITHDRAWN

JULIE SYKES
illustrated by LUCY TRUMAN

A STEPPING STONE BOOK™
Random House 🏠 New York

Text copyright © 2020 by Julie Sykes and Linda Chapman
Cover art and interior illustrations copyright © 2020 by Lucy Truman

Visit us on the Web! rhcbooks.com

Educators and librarians, for a variety of teaching tools, visit us at
RHTeachersLibrarians.com

Library of Congress Cataloging-in-Publication Data
Names: Sykes, Julie, author. | Truman, Lucy, illustrator.
Title: Isla and Buttercup / Julie Sykes ; illustrated by Lucy Truman.
Description: First American edition. | New York : Random House
Children's Books, [2021] | Series: Unicorn Academy ; 12 |
"A Stepping Stone Book." |
Summary: Isla and her unicorn, Buttercup, have not yet bonded so they
cannot graduate with their friends, but everything could change after they use
Buttercup's newly discovered finding magic to locate the evil Ms. Willow.
Identifiers: LCCN 2020055512 (print) | LCCN 2020055513 (ebook) |
ISBN 978-0-593-30788-5 (trade pbk.) | ISBN 978-0-593-30790-8 (lib. bdg.) |
ISBN 978-0-593-30789-2 (ebook)
Subjects: CYAC: Unicorns—Fiction. | Magic—Fiction. | Friendship—Fiction. |
Graduation (School)—Fiction. | Boarding schools—Fiction. |
Schools—Fiction.
Classification: LCC PZ7.S98325 Iu 2021 (print) | LCC PZ7.S98325 (ebook) |
DDC [Fic]—dc23

Printed in the United States of America
10 9 8 7 6 5 4 3
First American Edition

To Isla Rose Nicole–
may all your days be filled with magic.

CHAPTER 1

"Oh wow! That's amazing, Matilda!" said Isla. Matilda from Diamond dorm had covered the back wall of the stables with paper and was drawing a huge mural that showed the past year at Unicorn Academy. There were pictures of everyone arriving on the first day, being paired with their unicorns, galloping through the grounds, and camping in the woods. The other girls from Diamond dorm— Rosa, Freya, Ariana, and Violet—were painting the background, while Unibot, the robotic unicorn that Freya built, was helping the girls by rolling around with cans of paint.

"It does look good, doesn't it?" said Rosa.

Isla nodded. "I bet the parents will love it!"

Every student who'd bonded with their unicorn—who'd discovered their magic power—was about to graduate. In just a few days, all the

students' and unicorns' parents would come to the academy for the graduation ball. Students who weren't graduating, like Isla, would watch the ceremony, go home for Christmas, and return for a second year in January.

Matilda looked around. "Do you want to help us, Isla?"

Isla shook her head. "I'd only mess it up."

"Don't be silly. I'm no good at painting, so I'm just doing the grass," said Violet. "Join me!"

It looked like fun, but Isla didn't want to risk ruining their beautiful mural. "It's okay," she said cheerfully. "The others from my dorm will be here soon. We're making snowflakes to hang from the ceiling." She grinned. "That's about my level when it comes to art!"

"Come and sit with us anyway," said Violet, waving Isla over with a paintbrush.

Isla smiled again. "Thanks." The Diamond

dorm girls were always so friendly to her. She was going to miss them when they all graduated.

The girls in her dorm, Ruby dorm, didn't get along as well as Diamond dorm. Molly and Anna were nice, but they were best friends who did everything together. The fourth member of Ruby dorm, Valentina, had rich parents who were trustees at the school, and she acted like she was better than everyone else.

I wonder who will be in my dorm next year, Isla thought as she settled down to work on her snowflake. She wasn't sure how she felt about returning to the academy on her own. At least Buttercup, her confident, energetic unicorn, would be with her.

"We've been trying to think of where Ms. Willow could be hiding," said Violet. "Do you have any ideas?"

Ms. Willow had been the school nurse, until Diamond dorm discovered that she'd been draining magic from around the island as part of an evil plan to take it over! A month ago, Ms. Willow had kidnapped Violet and her unicorn, Twinkle, and had taken them to the Frozen Lagoon, where she was storing all the magic in the water under the ice. Thanks to Isla, the Diamond dorm girls had gone to Violet and Twinkle's rescue, and they'd all escaped. Now Ms. Willow had vanished without a trace.

"She might have gone back to the Frozen Lagoon," said Isla. Her face reddened as everyone turned to look at her. She hadn't meant to voice that aloud. Would they all think it was a silly idea?

"Of course! That must be it!" said Violet.

"You're so smart, Isla," said Matilda.

Isla turned even redder. "I don't know. I bet everyone else has better ideas."

Rosa grinned at her. "You shouldn't put yourself down. Your thought was actually really smart. Ms. Willow is bound to be hiding at the Frozen Lagoon. She's got lots of magic stored there, and it's a secret place that no one else knows how to get to."

"So how do we catch her if she's there?" said Freya.

Just then, Molly, Anna, and Valentina arrived carrying paper and scissors.

"Ooh, I like your snowflake, Isla!" said Molly.

Anna nodded. "Can you show me how you made it?"

Isla felt a sudden tingle of happiness, but it was quickly squashed by Valentina.

"It's too big," she said with a swish of her long dark hair. "And it's weird."

"Don't listen to her, Isla!" Rosa turned to Valentina. "That was a really mean thing to say!"

Valentina looked surprised. "But the cutouts are weird in parts."

"So? No one will notice when it's hanging up," said Freya.

"I actually think it'll be good to have snowflakes of all different sizes," added Molly.

"We've got some glue and glitter over here, Isla," Matilda called. "Why don't you start decorating the one you made?"

"Can we help?" Anna asked Isla.

Anna and Molly got glue and glitter and sat down with Isla to decorate the snowflake.

Valentina gave them a funny look. "What about me?" she said. "What am I going to do?"

No one answered her.

Valentina huffed and started to draw some

snowflakes on her own. Isla glanced over at her. She just didn't understand why Valentina said the things she did. If she wanted to have friends, why didn't she try harder to be more likable? Valentina was in her second year at the academy, and although her unicorn Golden Briar had discovered that he had wind magic, the two of them still hadn't bonded. Valentina would be the only student staying for a third year.

I'd hate that, thought Isla, feeling a sudden rush of sympathy for her. *If it were me, I'd do anything to graduate with everyone else.*

Just then, there was a clatter of hooves and the unicorns came trotting into the stables. They had been outside in the meadow, enjoying the winter sun.

"We want to go for a cross-country ride," Whisper, Ariana's unicorn, announced.

"We won't have many more chances to all be together," said Honey, Freya's unicorn.

"Can we go too?" Buttercup asked. She trotted over to Isla and nuzzled her as everyone started putting the art equipment down. Buttercup was a very pretty little unicorn with a pink-yellow-and-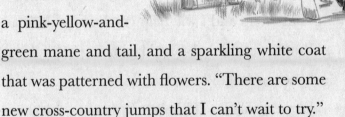green mane and tail, and a sparkling white coat that was patterned with flowers. "There are some new cross-country jumps that I can't wait to try."

"They're not too high for you, are they?" Isla asked. Buttercup was one of the smallest unicorns.

"Nothing's too high for me!" Buttercup declared.

The others were already leaving the stables. But Isla noticed that Freya was searching the ground and Honey, her unicorn, was walking slowly around, her muzzle touching the floor.

"Did you lose something?" Isla asked.

"A tiny screw from Unibot." Freya frowned. "It's so small, but without it, Unibot can't travel backward. Look."

The robotic unicorn was now stuck in a corner, a basket of paint cans in its mouth.

"Buttercup and I will help you look," said Isla.

Buttercup nodded. She liked being helpful just as much as Isla did.

Freya smiled. "Thanks. It has to be here somewhere."

"Find the screw, find it!" Buttercup sang out while rapping a hoof in time to the beat.

There was a loud pop, and Isla saw a pink spark drift down to the floor.

"Oh!" said Buttercup in surprise. "Did you see that? What was it?"

"Is it your magic?" said Freya in excitement. "The first time Honey found her super-speed magic, pink sparks came from her hooves."

"Do that again, whatever it was you were doing," urged Honey.

"What, this?" Buttercup thumped her hoof on the floor. *"Find the screw! Find—!"* she chanted, breaking off as a flurry of pink sparkles swirled up from her hooves.

Isla couldn't believe what she was seeing. The sparkles twirled and danced, then rose up together to form an arrow. It quivered in the air, its tip pointing at a crack where the wall joined the floor.

Buttercup trotted over and peered into the crack. "Here's Freya's screw! I *did* find it!"

"You've got your magic!" squealed Isla,

throwing her arms around Buttercup's neck. "It's *finding* magic!"

"Awesome!" said Freya. "You'll be able to find things whenever they get lost."

Buttercup's eyes shone. "Let's go tell the others right away!"

CHAPTER 2

Freya and Isla vaulted onto their unicorns and galloped after the others. Isla was buzzing with excitement and couldn't wait to share the news that Buttercup had found her magic.

"Wait!" Buttercup whinnied to the other unicorns.

They slowed to a halt.

"What's up?" demanded Rosa. A look of alarm crossed her face. "It's not Ms. Willow, is it?"

"No, it's not Ms. Willow," said Freya.

"What is it, then?" said Violet.

"It's Buttercup!" Isla burst out. "She's just discovered her magic!"

She told them what had happened.

"It was amazing!" said Freya. "A magical arrow appeared in the air and pointed to where the missing screw was."

"That's fantastic, Isla!" Violet exclaimed.

"Finding magic's so cool!" said Isla, thinking of all the people she and Buttercup could help.

Valentina frowned. "Don't think that just because you've found Buttercup's magic you'll be able to graduate!" she snapped. "You've still got to bond, remember! Come on, Golden Briar. Let's go."

"But . . . ," Golden Briar said.

"Now!" exclaimed Valentina, clapping her heels against his sides. With a sigh, Golden Briar cantered away.

"She's so mean," said Matilda. "She could at least have congratulated you."

"Ignore her," said Violet. "I bet you'll bond really quickly and be able to graduate after all."

"Yep!" Buttercup said happily. "I bet we will too."

Isla patted Buttercup's neck as they rode on. She was very glad that her unicorn wasn't upset by Valentina's comments, but she couldn't help feeling a little worried. She'd been so excited to find Buttercup's magic, but of course they still might not graduate. *Oh, I hope we bond soon,* she thought. *I really do!*

They all had a great time on the cross-country course and returned to the stables talking and laughing. Golden Briar was already in his stall, next door to Buttercup's.

"Did you have fun?" he asked.

Buttercup nodded. "It was amazing! I jumped over a huge log pile."

"I wish I'd been able to come with you," said Golden Briar.

"Next time you should. Tell Valentina it's your turn to decide what you do. Isn't that right, Isla?" said Buttercup.

"Valentina often lets me do what I want," Golden Briar said firmly. He turned back to his hay net.

Isla suddenly felt sorry for Golden Briar—and for Valentina too. How would it feel not to have bonded after two years at the academy?

"Buttercup!" Matilda called out. "Can you use your magic to help me find my favorite blue pen? I lost it last week."

Buttercup lifted her head. "Coming!" She and Isla went to the Diamond dorm aisle. "Stand back, everyone!" Buttercup gave a big bow, clearly enjoying herself. She lifted her hoof, then smacked it down on the ground. "Find Matilda's blue pen!"

Everyone gasped as a rainbow of sparks shot

up and arched above her head. The arrow hung in the air for a second, then darted out through the stables' door.

"After it!" cried Buttercup. She cantered out of the stables, then skidded to a halt. "Whoops! Sorry, Isla! I almost forgot you!" Isla ran up to her and vaulted on. The others mounted their unicorns and cantered after the arrow.

It sailed over the stables' roof and into the meadow, stopping by the stream. Buttercup trotted over to where the arrow floated in the air, pointing at the reeds.

"I found your pen!" she exclaimed. She tossed her muzzle toward the reeds.

CLUCK!

With a flurry of wings, a pale blue bird burst from the reeds.

"Whaaa!" cried Buttercup, stumbling backward in shock.

Rosa laughed. "Your magic found a blue *hen*, not Matilda's blue *pen*, Buttercup!"

Isla turned hot with embarrassment for Buttercup as everyone laughed, but Buttercup laughed just as loudly as the others.

"Oh dear!" she snorted. "I think I need to practice a bit more."

"Don't worry," said Violet. "Most unicorns find it hard to control their magic when they first discover their powers."

Matilda's unicorn, Pearl, nodded in agreement. "I found it really hard to hold glamours at first."

The other unicorns nodded too. "You get tired easily as well," said Twinkle. "But it gets better the more you practice."

"I'll practice lots, then!" declared Buttercup. She nuzzled Isla. "You'll help me, won't you?"

"Of course," said Isla, leaning in to bury her face in Buttercup's long pink-yellow-and-green mane. When they bonded, a strand of her brown hair would turn the same colors. *Oh, please make that happen soon,* Isla thought again.

CHAPTER 3

After lunch, Isla went to look for Ms. Nettles to tell her about Buttercup's finding magic. The head teacher's study door was shut, and there was no answer when Isla knocked. Ms. Rosemary, the Care of Unicorns teacher, looked out of her room. "Are you looking for Ms. Nettles, Isla?"

Isla nodded. "Buttercup found her magic this morning."

"That's wonderful news!" said Ms. Rosemary. "But I'm afraid Ms. Nettles was called away last night on urgent business. I'm sure she'll be happy

to hear about Buttercup's magic when she gets back, though."

Isla smiled and headed to the stables.

"Can we practice my magic?" asked Buttercup when Isla arrived. "Please!" she added, fluttering her eyelashes.

Isla grinned. "Of course we can."

"Yay! Miki lost his ball last week, and Golden Briar wants me to find Valentina's favorite scarf, and Monsoon said Ms. Bramble lost—"

"Whoa!" said Isla, holding her hands up. "Maybe we should just find one thing at a time!"

"Oh, okay," Buttercup said with a huff. "We'll start with Miki's ball, then. He was on the field when he lost it."

They went out to the field. Buttercup took a deep breath. "Miki's ball!" she exclaimed. "Find

21

it!" The magic flew in a circle, then started moving away.

"My magic's working! Yippee!" said Buttercup as she raced after it.

The arrow flew in the direction of Sparkle Lake. But as it got closer, it moved from side to side, as if it couldn't decide which way to go. Buttercup galloped after it. Isla held on to her mane. "Slow down, Buttercup!" she cried.

The arrow flew over the fountain, then moved to the right and pointed at some bushes close to the water. It stayed there for a second before it shot to a nearby bush, then flew back to the fountain.

Buttercup's ears flicked, and she increased her speed.

"No, Buttercup!" Isla gasped. "We can't follow it into the lake! Stop!"

The arrow suddenly returned to the bush. Buttercup turned to go after it, but she was

galloping too fast. Her hooves slid from under her. Isla shrieked as they skidded toward the rainbow water.

SPLASH!

Buttercup's hooves hit the lake, and a wave of ice cold water splashed over them. Luckily, Buttercup just managed to stop herself from falling in completely.

"Whoops!" Buttercup regained her balance. "Are you okay, Isla?"

"Well, I'm pretty wet," said Isla, shivering. She had water dripping from her hair, and drops were already freezing on her clothes.

"Sorry!" said Buttercup. "I was just trying to catch up with the arrow." She looked around. "Oh, it's gone," she said in disappointment.

"Why was it jumping around like that?" Isla asked.

"I don't know. It pointed at the bush before it

vanished. Maybe Miki's ball is there." Buttercup trotted toward it.

"Wait! There's something in those bushes," said Isla, spotting a flash of color.

Buttercup went over. "Valentina's scarf!" she said, pulling the scarf out of the rushes with her teeth. Isla leaned over her neck and took it from her.

"Valentina will be happy to have it back. I wonder why the arrow pointed to the scarf when we were looking for Miki's ball."

Buttercup frowned. "I guess I was thinking about both things at the same time—the ball and the scarf. Maybe it confused my magic. Let's see if there's anything in the bush." She cantered over. "Miki's ball! Hooray!" Buttercup nudged it out with her nose. "Look! I found both things!"

Isla hesitated. She didn't want to hurt Buttercup's feelings. "That's great, but you need to practice controlling your magic. Maybe you should concentrate on one thing at a time?"

"I think I did very well," said Buttercup, a little huffily.

Isla patted her neck. "You did, but let's start with small things first."

"I don't need to," Buttercup said confidently. "I'm super good already!"

"Let's go get you some sky berries," said Isla, changing the subject. Doing magic used up a unicorn's strength, and sky berries helped them recover.

"Okay, I guess I am a bit tired," admitted Buttercup.

They headed back to the stables. As they passed

the playground, they saw Rosa, Matilda, Freya, Ariana, Violet, and their unicorns by the swings.

"Shall we say hello?" said Buttercup.

Isla wasn't sure. "It looks like they might be having a private talk."

"So? They'll want to see us!" said Buttercup. "They're our friends!" She cantered over.

"Hi, everyone! What are you talking about?" she whinnied.

Isla panicked. "It's okay," she said quickly. "You don't have to tell us if it's a secret."

"Don't be silly. We don't have secrets from you two," said Violet. "We were just talking again about how we might find Ms. Willow."

Rosa looked at them thoughtfully. "Buttercup, do you think you could use your magic to find her?"

"I bet I could," said Buttercup.

"Great!" said Rosa. "Will you try?"

Buttercup nodded eagerly.

"Are you sure, Buttercup?" Isla asked. "I think you should practice more and rest before you try something so difficult."

Buttercup looked hurt. "Don't you believe in me, Isla?"

"Yes, but—"

"I found the ball and the scarf, didn't I?" said Buttercup.

"Yes, but we almost fell into the lake!" Isla reminded her.

"That was just a silly mistake." Buttercup looked upset now.

"Maybe this isn't such a good idea," said Ariana. "Ms. Willow is very smart. After all, she captured Prancer, and Prancer is a spell weaver." A spell weaver was the most powerful of unicorns. Ms. Willow had braided magic ribbons into Prancer's mane to force her

to do whatever she commanded. "It could be dangerous."

"It'll be fine!" Buttercup tossed her mane. "I know I can do it. Just watch and see!"

Buttercup hit the ground with her hoof. "Find Ms. Willow!"

A few sparks spun in the air. They fizzled away.

"Find her!" Buttercup repeated, stamping both hooves so hard that she dislodged some mud that shot up and splattered her face. Violet giggled.

"Find her!" said Buttercup once more, but this time no sparks appeared at all.

"Oh." Buttercup looked disappointed.

Isla felt awful for her.

Violet gave her a kind look. "Don't worry, Buttercup. Isla's right—you're probably too tired after finding all the other stuff."

"Maybe I do need sky berries to get my strength back," Buttercup said.

"We can always try again tomorrow," said Rosa.

CHAPTER 4

"Sky berries for all the unicorns and hot chocolate for us!" said Matilda happily.

"I have some marshmallows for the hot chocolate," said Ariana.

"You'll have some hot chocolate with us, won't you, Isla?" Violet said.

Isla was thrilled to be included. "Yes, please!"

They rode back to the stables. Isla was happy to be with everyone, but she had an anxious feeling that Buttercup was upset with her.

I didn't mean to hurt her feelings, Isla thought. *I just didn't want her to look silly in front of everyone.*

"Isn't that Valentina?" said Freya, interrupting Isla's thoughts. "Where's she going?"

"Let's give her scarf back," said Isla. "I bet she'll be really happy we found it for her." Buttercup cantered toward Golden Briar.

"Valentina!" called Isla.

"Go away!" Valentina shouted at Isla.

"But I have something of yours."

"What is it?" demanded Valentina, slowing Golden Briar down.

Isla took the scarf out of her pocket. "Buttercup used her magic to find it."

Valentina took the scarf from Isla and stuffed it into her pocket. She didn't even say thank you.

"Where are you going?" asked Isla.

"None of your business!" snapped Valentina, and she rode away without another word.

"I was only trying to help," Isla said to Buttercup as they headed back to the stables.

"Well, not everyone wants your help," said Buttercup. "I felt bad earlier when you said my magic wouldn't work."

"But I was right," Isla pointed out. "You were too tired."

"So what? It's better to try something and fail than not to try at all."

Isla wasn't sure she agreed. Surely it was better not to try if you thought you might get it wrong?

Buttercup got quiet. Isla hadn't meant to upset her. She'd only tried to stop her from using her magic because she knew that if *she'd* tried something and gotten it wrong, she'd be really embarrassed. Buttercup was different, though. She didn't mind making mistakes. *It's one of the things I love about her,* Isla realized. *She's so confident. She doesn't care what people think.*

As they reached the stables, Isla stroked Buttercup's neck. "I'm sorry. I didn't mean to

make you feel silly. You're right. It is better to try things than be too scared to try, like me."

Buttercup nuzzled her. "You just worry too much. I'm really glad we're paired together."

"Me too." Isla kissed her, then fetched a bucket full of juicy sky berries.

Buttercup gave her a friendly nudge.

"Friends again?" Isla said hopefully.

"Always friends," said Buttercup.

Isla hugged her, feeling much more cheerful.

Isla had fun with the others in Diamond dorm sipping hot chocolate, and she was bursting with happiness as she ran back to Ruby dorm to get ready for dinner. The only person in there was Valentina. She was reading a letter and frowning.

"News from home?" Isla asked.

Valentina shook her head and shoved the letter into her dresser, dropping the envelope in her

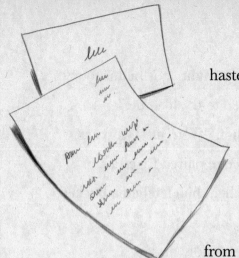

haste. Isla picked it up for her. It had Valentina's name on it in swirly handwriting, and no other address.

Valentina snatched it from her and slammed the drawer shut. She sat on her bed as Isla changed into a clean shirt and pulled a brush through her short hair.

"Aren't you going down to dinner?" Isla asked.

"I'm waiting for you," said Valentina.

Isla blinked. Valentina never waited for anyone. A thought crossed her mind. *Maybe Valentina was worried she would read her letter. Was it from a secret admirer or something?*

"I'm not ready," said Isla, deciding to test her theory.

"How long does it take to brush your hair?" Valentina asked. "Hurry up. All of Ruby dorm looks bad if one of us is late." She went to snatch the hairbrush away, but Isla held on to it.

"I said I'm not ready yet," Isla said.

Valentina glared at her. "You're so annoying."

Isla continued to slowly brush her hair while Valentina waited, her foot tapping on the floor.

Interesting, thought Isla. Valentina usually flounced off if she didn't get her way. What was she hiding?

CHAPTER 5

Isla and Buttercup decided to meet Diamond dorm in the barn next to the stables before breakfast to try Buttercup's finding magic again. When Isla woke up, Molly and Anna were still sleeping, but Valentina's bed was empty. Where could she be?

As Isla left the dorm, she spotted a white envelope on the floor that had been pushed under their door. It had Valentina's name on it, in exactly the same handwriting as the one Isla saw the day before.

Isla's eyes widened. Did Valentina have a secret

36

admirer? Was that who the letters were from? Biting back a giggle, she put the envelope on Valentina's bedside table.

As Isla entered the stables, Valentina poked her head out of Golden Briar's stall. "What are you doing here?" she asked.

"Oh . . . I'm just doing something with Diamond dorm," Isla said.

"Is it time already?" Buttercup asked, looking over her stall door.

"Is it time for what?" said Valentina.

"Nothing," said Isla. "Nothing at all."

"Ready when you are, Isla!" called Rosa.

Isla got Buttercup out of her stall.

Valentina followed them up the aisle. "What are you all doing? Can I come too?" she asked.

"No," Rosa spoke bluntly. "You don't like us, and we don't really like you, either."

Isla wished Rosa had sounded nicer, but

37

Valentina had been mean to Matilda in the past and Rosa was a good friend.

"Fine!" Valentina said. "I bet you're doing something silly anyway!" She stomped back into Golden Briar's stall.

Isla joined the others as they cantered to the barn.

"Are you ready to do your magic, Buttercup?" Matilda said.

"Definitely!" said Buttercup. "It's going to work this time. I know it is!"

"Go, Buttercup!" said Ariana.

"Stand back, everyone," said Buttercup, clearly loving being the center of attention. "Here goes!"

She stomped on the ground dramatically. "Find Ms. Willow!" Sparks swirled around her hoof, twirling up in the air to form a quivering, colored arrow.

Matilda squealed in excitement.

Buttercup shot Isla a smug look as the arrow floated toward the barn door.

"Go!" cried Isla, leaping onto Buttercup's back as the arrow began to gather speed.

She heard the whoops and cries of the others as they thundered behind her. Isla leaned forward, enjoying the wind on her face as they galloped.

"Where's it going?" she cried to Buttercup as the arrow turned toward the vegetable gardens.

"I don't know!" said Buttercup.

The arrow reached a large compost heap that stood beside a worn brick building at the bottom of the garden. It had a tree beside it, with branches that drooped down gracefully to the ground. The

door was slightly open. The arrow hovered above the shed, pointing at it.

Buttercup skidded to a stop.

"Why's the arrow pointing at the shed?" said Rosa.

Freya gasped. "Maybe Ms. Willow is inside!"

They all looked at each other in alarm.

"What should we do?" whispered Matilda.

Just then, the door moved. They all froze. Something the size of an apple, with eight legs and googly eyes, came scuttling out. Ariana shrieked, but the rest of them sighed with relief.

"It's just a cave spider!" exclaimed Violet as the spider ran past them and up the tree trunk.

"The tree!" Freya pointed. "It's a weeping willow. That must be why the arrow brought us here. Buttercup, you found a *willow tree*, not Ms. Willow!"

They all burst out laughing.

"Whoops!" said Buttercup.

"What's going on here, girls?"

Ms. Nettles came out of the shed, her glasses rattling on the end of her bony nose. The arrow exploded in a shower of sparkles that faded like a firework.

The girls stopped laughing instantly as the head teacher looked at them sternly, one hand on her hip. "Ms. Nettles!" Rosa exclaimed in shock.

"Why are you all up so early?" Ms. Nettles asked.

"Erm . . . We were . . . out looking for sparkle moss," Matilda said.

Violet nodded. "To decorate the ballroom for graduation day."

Ms. Nettles frowned. "Sparkle moss grows near water. I would try by the lake and stay away from here. This building isn't safe."

"We'll go to the lake right away," said Freya.

Isla remembered something. "Ms. Nettles, Buttercup's got finding magic!" she said excitedly.

"Really?" said Ms. Nettles, raising her eyebrows. "Well, if her magic brought her here to find sparkle moss, she clearly needs more practice." She shooed at them with her hands. "Go on. Away with you all."

Isla's face fell, and she saw Buttercup's ears droop.

"She could at least have said well done," said Violet indignantly as they walked away.

"We probably just caught her at a bad time," said Isla, but she couldn't help feeling upset that Ms. Nettles hadn't seemed happier for her and Buttercup. "I didn't even realize she'd come back. Ms. Rosemary said she'd been called away on urgent business. I wonder why she was in the shed?"

"Studying the cave spider maybe," said Freya. "She does love nature."

"Or collecting more beetles," added Violet. Ms. Nettles had a large collection of beetles.

Ariana shuddered. "I don't understand why anyone would want to collect beetles!"

"I like beetles," said Whisper, Ariana's unicorn. Whisper had soothing magic and loved all animals.

At Sparkle Lake, they collected some sparkle moss, just in case Ms. Nettles checked up on them, before returning to the stables. As Isla passed

Golden Briar's stall, she heard Valentina talking to him in a low voice.

"I don't know what to do. The person writing them says they need my help. I think the writer might be—" She broke off quickly as she saw Isla and Buttercup.

"Were you listening to our private conversation?" Valentina demanded.

For a second, Isla thought she saw a flash of fear in Valentina's eyes. "No!" she said. "Of course I wasn't!" She wondered why Valentina looked so worried about being overheard. Who did she think was sending her the letters? A horrible thought suddenly filled Isla's mind. Could it be Ms. Willow? Why else would Valentina look so upset?

Valentina pointed at the moss Isla was carrying. "You were up early just to collect sparkle moss?"

"No, we didn't go out to just get moss," said Isla without thinking. Too late, she realized she'd said too much.

"Why *were* you out so early, then?" Valentina asked. "What were you and Diamond dorm doing?"

"Um . . . ," Isla stammered. "It was, um . . . nothing."

"Tell me!" said Valentina. She lowered her voice again. "Is it something to do with Ms. Willow?"

Isla's heart pounded. What had made Valentina jump to that conclusion? Maybe her thoughts about the writer of Valentina's mysterious letters *were* correct! "Ms. Willow? No!" she said, hoping she sounded convincing.

"If it is, I want to help," said Valentina, her voice suddenly very serious. "I really do. Tell me what's going on. *Please!*"

Isla opened and shut her mouth. She hated leaving Valentina out, but she didn't really trust her. Anyway, the secret wasn't hers to tell. "I . . . I can't say," she said.

Valentina's face hardened. "Fine! Be like that! If you don't want my help, then you won't have it!" She left the stall and stomped away.

CHAPTER 6

After lunch, Isla met with Diamond dorm in the barn. She'd been thinking over and over about her conversation with Valentina, and what she'd heard Valentina saying to Golden Briar. She had a very bad feeling. She wondered whether to say anything to the others, but she had no proof that the letters were from Ms. Willow. What if she told them and it wasn't true? She'd feel so embarrassed!

"So how *are* we going to find Ms. Willow?" said Freya. "If she is at the Frozen Lagoon, she's going to be impossible to find. No one knows its location, and it's not marked on the magic map."

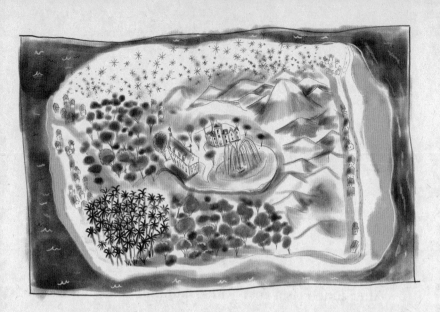

The magic map was an exact copy of Unicorn Island that was kept in the Great Hall. If the map thought you wanted to help, it would magically transport you anywhere on the island that you asked it to.

"We could use my magic again," Buttercup said. "I could ask it to find the Frozen Lagoon."

"You could," said Ariana carefully. "But if the magic map isn't powerful enough to show us where the Frozen Lagoon is, then I'm not sure your magic will be able to help, Buttercup."

Buttercup looked a little upset. "Don't you think I can find Ms. Willow?"

"Maybe you should practice a bit more first," said Violet quickly. "Soon your magic will be stronger, and then you can try again."

"If there's time," said Freya. "We've only got a couple of days left until graduation."

"We need another plan," said Rosa.

They kept thinking, but by the end of lunchtime, they still didn't have any idea how to get to the Frozen Lagoon. Isla went back to her dorm to get ready for her afternoon lessons and saw another envelope on Valentina's bed.

Isla picked the envelope up and glanced across at Valentina's dresser. A drawer was half-open, and she could see other letters inside. She knew she shouldn't look, but no one was around. What if they *were* from Ms. Willow? *I'll just look at a few lines,* Isla thought. Feeling a little

guilty, Isla picked up the top letter and scanned it.

You're so much smarter than all the other students, Valentina. You understand how things work. You know I want to make Unicorn Island better, and you are the one student who can help me. In return, I will help you and Golden Briar graduate. Think about it, Valentina. That is what you want most in the world, isn't it?

There was no name or signature on the bottom.

Hearing footsteps on the stairs, Isla shoved the letter back into the drawer and ran to her bed. She picked up her hairbrush as Molly, Anna, and Valentina walked in. Isla's mind spun. Who were the letters from, and what did they mean?

Valentina picked up the new envelope from her pillow. She quickly opened and read it, then shoved it into the drawer with the others. She sat down on her bed, facing away from Isla.

"Are you okay?" asked Isla.

"Why wouldn't I be?" Valentina said sharply.

"Who was your letter from?"

"None of your business!" Valentina glared at her. "You won't share your secrets with me, so I won't share mine with you!"

Not fair! thought Isla. *I'm trying to protect Unicorn Island. Can you say the same?*

The bell rang, and everyone left together to go to afternoon lessons. Isla pretended that she'd forgotten her pencil case and ran back to the dorm. When she got there, she pulled out the letter Valentina had just received from the top of the pile. It simply read:

Tonight, I want to help you. It is time to prove your loyalty.

A bad feeling shivered down Isla's spine. *What should I do?* she thought. *If I tell the others, they might ask Valentina and she'll find out that I've read her letters. And what if it ends up being nothing?*

Isla hesitated a moment longer, before pushing

the letter back into the drawer and running to her lesson.

Later, as Isla got ready to practice the drill ride her dorm would perform in front of the parents, she watched Valentina through the fence that separated Buttercup's stall from Golden Briar's. Valentina was whispering, and Golden Briar was shaking his head quickly. Isla moved closer to the fence.

"We've got to go, Golden Briar," she heard Valentina say.

"No, Valentina, we can't!"

"But this could be our only chance to—"

"What's up, Isla?" Buttercup called out. "Why are you standing over there?"

"No reason," said Isla, hurrying back to her. She thought about what Valentina had said: *We've got to go.* Go where? She bit her lip. If the letters

52

were from Ms. Willow, did that mean Valentina was planning on meeting her? Another shiver ran down her spine as she remembered the letter she had read: *Tonight, I want to help you. It is time to prove your loyalty.*

"Are you sure you're okay?" Buttercup nudged her. "You seem distracted."

Isla bit her lip. "Buttercup, if you had a feeling that someone was going to make a really big mistake, would it be right to tell your friends? Even if there was a chance you were wrong?" Isla suddenly realized she trusted Buttercup's thoughts. Their opinions were very different, but together that made them stronger.

"You should definitely tell your friends," said Buttercup immediately. "Imagine if you didn't and something bad happened. You'd feel awful. If the person has nothing to hide, then they

shouldn't mind explaining themselves. I think it's better to look silly than to let someone make a big mistake."

Isla hugged her. "You're right. Thank you. I'm so lucky to have you as my unicorn."

"And I'm lucky to have you as my rider!" Buttercup said, nuzzling her.

CHAPTER 7

Isla and Buttercup left the stables to go to the drill ride practice.

I'll tell Diamond dorm about Valentina's letters as soon as I get a chance to speak to everyone alone, thought Isla.

Diamond dorm was ahead of her, laughing with the boys from Topaz dorm as Matilda and Miki tried to trip each other.

Ms. Nettles came marching toward the stables. "Matilda! Stop that this instant!" she shouted.

"Sorry," said Matilda.

"It was my fault too, sorry," said Miki.

Ms. Nettles ignored him. "Matilda, you will not

ride this afternoon. Instead you'll write out *I must behave more appropriately* a hundred times."

Matilda gaped in shock. "But . . . I said sorry, and we're about to practice the drill ride. . . ."

"Silence. Or I shall make that two hundred times!"

Isla and Violet looked at each other, shocked. The teachers were all uptight about finding Ms. Willow, especially Ms. Nettles, but she was never this unfair. Matilda looked like she was about to cry.

"Please, Ms. Nettles. We have so little time left to practice," Rosa begged. "Can't Matilda do lines later?"

"One hundred lines for all of Diamond dorm!" Ms. Nettles barked.

Everyone gasped.

Ms. Nettles looked around. "Anyone else?" she asked. No one dared to move. She nodded. "Diamond dorm, take your unicorns back and go inside now. The rest of you get practicing. Oh, and, Valentina?"

"Yes?" Valentina looked at her nervously. Ms. Nettles was her aunt, but she never gave Valentina special attention.

"I would like you to have the star role in the drill ride."

Valentina blinked. "But I'm not ready to graduate." Isla knew that at the start of the year, Valentina would have loved to have a main role.

Now she looked almost upset. "Shouldn't I just do what everyone else does?" Valentina went on.

Ms. Nettles smiled at her. "Always so modest, Valentina. No, you deserve this role. Come to my study right after dinner, and we'll talk about it." She turned and walked away.

As soon as Ms. Nettles was out of earshot everyone started to talk at once.

"What's going on?" hissed Himmat from Topaz dorm. "I've never known the Nettle Patch to be so prickly!"

"It's not fair," said Miki. "I should be in as much trouble as Matilda, and Ms. Nettles didn't give me lines."

"I'm sure she'll give you some if you want," said Jake with a grin. "Just go ask her."

"Maybe not," said Miki, rolling his eyes. "But I do feel bad for Diamond dorm."

Isla glanced at Valentina. Did *she* know why

her aunt was in such a bad mood? Valentina
looked up.

"What are you staring at?" she demanded.

"Nothing," Isla said hurriedly.

When afternoon lessons were over, Isla went to
the barn to meet up with Diamond dorm. "Did
you get your lines done?" she asked them.

They all nodded.

"I still don't understand why Ms. Nettles was so
mean," said Violet.

"It was very weird," Rosa agreed, "but we're
here to talk about Ms. Willow and how we're
going to find her. We're running out of time."

Isla felt suddenly hot. This was her chance to
tell the others what was going on with Valentina.
But now the moment was here, doubts filled her
mind again. What if she'd made a huge mistake?

"The good thing is, Ms. Willow can't get onto

the school grounds," said Ariana. "The teachers put protection spells on the boundaries to keep her out."

Isla hesitated. If Ms. Willow couldn't get onto the grounds, then how could Valentina be planning on meeting her? Ms. Willow couldn't be the mystery letter writer after all. Isla swallowed and kept silent.

After dinner, Isla left the table at the same time as Valentina.

"We're going to the barn with the unicorns," said Violet as Isla passed her. "Are you coming?"

"I'll join you in a bit," said Isla. Valentina had been strangely quiet at dinner, and Isla wanted to see if she could find out why. Maybe Valentina had gotten another letter?

As Isla followed Valentina up the stairs, Ms. Nettles appeared. "There you are, Valentina. Are

you ready for our meeting? I hope so. Tonight, I want to help you."

Valentina smiled as she and Ms. Nettles went down the teachers' hall together. Something bothered Isla as she watched them. What was it?

Tonight, I want to help you.

The words echoed in her head. They were the exact same words from Valentina's mystery letters. Ms. Nettles wasn't the letter writer, was she?

Isla hurried along the hall, tiptoeing the last few steps up to Ms. Nettles's study. The door was slightly open, and she could hear Valentina's voice.

"You might as well stop pretending. I know you're not my aunt!" she heard her say.

Isla's eyes widened.

"Clever girl," a voice purred. "I knew I was right to trust you and send you those letters!

You're so much smarter than everyone else, Valentina. How did I give myself away?"

"My aunt would never give me special treatment like you did over the graduation display ride," said Valentina. "So who are you?"

There was a faint flash of light. Isla pressed her eye to the crack in the door and smothered a squeak. Ms. Willow was suddenly standing in Ms. Nettles's study!

CHAPTER 8

"Ms. Willow!" exclaimed Valentina. "I knew you were the one sending the letters. And when my aunt started behaving strangely today, I guessed it wasn't really her but you in disguise!" Isla was surprised that she didn't sound scared. "How did you disguise yourself and get around the protection spells?" Valentina asked.

"Prancer cast a glamour, making me look like Ms. Nettles. As for the protection spells"—Ms. Willow waved a hand—"with the magic I've stored in the lagoon and with Prancer's powers, they were easy to break."

"Where is my aunt?" asked Valentina, and now Isla was sure she heard her voice shake.

"Safely out of the way, trapped in a secret place. I sent her a letter inviting her to an urgent meeting about Ms. Willow, and I captured her and her unicorn as she left the school. Now I shall bind all the unicorns in this school to me! They shall become my army and help me take over the island!"

"How?" said Valentina.

Ms. Willow laughed and clapped her hands in delight. "A girl after my own heart. Always asking questions. There is enough magic stored in the Frozen Lagoon to make binding ribbons for every unicorn at the academy. Once the ribbons are in their manes, they will obey me, just as Prancer does!"

Isla's heart pounded as Valentina chuckled. "So where do I come into all of this and, more

importantly, what do I get in return?"

"Money, power, and, of course, you'll get to graduate from the academy. Not that you'll need to after tomorrow night. First, you must prove your loyalty by binding Golden Briar to you. Then we shall work together to bind all the unicorns. We can do this if we work together. What do you say?"

Say no, Isla thought fiercely. *Don't agree!*

Her stomach sank as she heard Valentina say firmly, "Yes, I'll do it."

"I knew I had made the right choice!" said Ms. Willow. "Get Golden Briar, then meet me by the

lake. Do not breathe a word of this to anyone, especially Golden Briar. Once he is bound to you, my quest—*our* quest—to take over Unicorn Island will begin!"

Isla couldn't listen anymore. She raced up to the teachers' lounge, but she slowed down as she got closer. What if none of the teachers believed her? She didn't have any proof. They might just send her away, or even worse, they might laugh at her.

So what should she do?

Diamond dorm! If she told them, they would help her convince the teachers. She was sure of it!

Remembering that they were going to the barn, Isla charged back along the hall and out into the dark night. As she got closer to the barn, she heard laughter coming from it. She had just reached the door when she caught a movement from the corner of her eye—it was Valentina leading Golden Briar out of the stables.

Isla felt a rush of anger. How could Valentina be evil enough to work with Ms. Willow?

"Valentina!" she yelled, changing direction and running straight toward her roommate. But Valentina didn't hear her. She vaulted onto Golden Briar's back and cantered straight toward the lake—and Ms. Willow.

Isla charged after her, as fast as she could. "Valentina! No!" she screamed.

CHAPTER 9

Isla ran faster than she'd ever run in her life. *I have to stop Valentina.* The thought drummed through her brain, over and over again. Getting closer to the lake, Isla saw Ms. Willow on a tall unicorn with a golden mane. Golden Briar had stopped next to Ms. Willow's unicorn, and Ms. Willow was smiling at Valentina and reaching for her hand.

"Come with me, my dear."

"I didn't realize we were going somewhere." Isla thought she could hear an edge to Valentina's voice. "Where are you taking me?"

"To the Frozen Lagoon!" Ms. Willow's fingers closed on Valentina's.

"No!" shrieked Isla, bursting out of the shadows and grabbing Valentina's foot.

For a second, she saw Valentina's and Ms. Willow's shocked faces, and then there was a flash of green and the world fell away. Isla spun around and around before dropping to the ground, landing with a thud on a glassy, freezing surface. The sky was packed with glittering stars. Isla blinked, realizing she was on a thick layer of ice above a lagoon that swirled beneath it. This had to be the Frozen Lagoon, where Ms. Willow was storing the island's stolen magic. Isla scrambled toward the bank.

"You!" Ms. Willow hissed. "What are *you* doing here?" She turned to Valentina. "Did you tell her about meeting me?"

"No!" Valentina exclaimed, looking at Isla in shock.

Ms. Willow flicked a bolt of magic at Isla. Isla cried out as it smacked into her and sent her flying across the lagoon. As she landed, all the breath was knocked out of her.

"Isla!" she heard Valentina cry.

"Ignore her!" snapped Ms. Willow. "She is no threat to us. I'll deal with her in a minute. Prancer, make sure she does not leave the ice until I am back." The golden-maned unicorn nodded. "I'll go and get the ribbons so that you can bind Golden Briar to prove your loyalty."

It was Valentina's turn to nod, and Isla felt a rush of anger as Ms. Willow marched toward a hut near the lagoon.

As soon as Ms. Willow disappeared inside, Valentina looked briefly to where Isla was getting to her feet. Then Valentina ran over to

70

Prancer. She pulled something from her pocket and grabbed Prancer's mane. Isla saw a flash of moonlight on metal.

"Valentina! Stop! Don't, whatever you're doing! You mustn't help Ms. Willow!" she cried.

"Help Ms. Willow?" Valentina spluttered. "For goodness' sake, Isla! As if I would!"

"What? You can't deny it!" said Isla. "She's getting the binding ribbons right now!"

"I had to agree so I could do this!" Valentina held up a pair of scissors and a clump of ribbons fell to the ground. "It was my plan all along."

"I'm free of

the binding!" whinnied Prancer, shaking her mane. "The ribbons are gone! Oh, thank you, Valentina!"

"Did you really believe that I would bind Golden Briar to me?" Valentina asked. "I'd never do that!"

"Oh!" Isla's eyes were wide as she hurried off the ice. "So you aren't working with Ms. Willow?"

"Don't be silly! I thought if she believed I was working with her, then I could find a way to *trap* her. I wasn't expecting her to bring me here, though!" said Valentina.

"It's true!" Golden Briar agreed. "I didn't want Valentina to meet her at first, but she insisted."

"I was sure I could find a way to stop her," said Valentina.

"Oh," said Isla, realizing she was wrong about Valentina. "I should have trusted you."

"Yes, you really should've!" said Valentina. She turned to Prancer. "Do you know where my aunt is, Prancer?"

"Ms. Willow shut her and her unicorn in a shed in the academy grounds before moving them here to a cave in the woods. I can show you the way there. Get on my back, Isla—it'll be faster if you ride."

Hardly able to believe her eyes, Isla scrambled off the ice and onto Prancer's back. She'd never ridden another unicorn before, and tall, strong Prancer felt very different from little Buttercup. Isla's heart twisted. She wished Buttercup was there with her. *But at least she's not in danger,* she thought as they began to gallop around the lagoon. She felt bad for not trusting Valentina earlier and for not telling the teachers about Ms. Willow when she'd had the chance. She shouldn't have worried about looking silly. She should have

74

just said something. She glanced behind her, half expecting to see Ms. Willow racing after them.

After a few minutes, Prancer skidded to a stop. "Ms. Nettles and Thyme are in that cave," she hissed, motioning toward an opening in the gray stone in front of them.

Three wolves were guarding the entrance. They lowered their heads and began to snarl. Their eyes glowed red.

"Ms. Willow enchanted them to attack anyone who gets too close," warned Prancer.

"Can you lift the enchantment?" asked Valentina.

"Not on my own. It takes both a spell-weaving unicorn and their partner to undo enchantment spells."

The wolves inched forward, their eyes fixed on the unicorns, their wide-open mouths revealing razor-sharp teeth.

Isla saw the
wolves' muscles
bunch. They
were about
to spring! She
tensed, and
then, suddenly, a little
unicorn came bursting out of the nearby trees
and charged at the wolves.

"Buttercup!" Isla shrieked, her head spinning.
What was her unicorn doing there?

"I won't let you hurt Isla! I won't!" whinnied
Buttercup, fiercely galloping straight toward the
snarling wolves!

CHAPTER 10

The lead wolf leaped at Buttercup. Isla screamed as she saw its open mouth and its sharp fangs, but a second later, it was flying sideways through the air. It landed with a howl, Freya and Honey standing beside it. Using Honey's super-speed, they'd galloped straight into the wolf, knocking it off target.

"Way to go, Freya and Honey!" cried Rosa as she appeared from the trees with Violet, Ariana, and Matilda.

"Isla! I'm so glad you're all right," Buttercup said, racing over to her. "We were in the barn when

I heard you shout at Valentina outside. When I went to the door, I saw you running toward the lake. I galloped after you and got there just as you grabbed Valentina and disappeared with her and Ms. Willow! What's going on?"

"Oh, Buttercup!" Isla jumped down from Prancer to bury her face in Buttercup's mane. "Thank you for coming after me." Being with her unicorn was all that mattered!

"I always want to be by your side when you're in danger," said Buttercup.

"And I want to be by yours," said Isla, hugging her.

Ariana's voice brought her back to reality. "You did it, Whisper!"

Glancing around, Isla saw that Whisper had used her calming magic to free the wolves. The red had died from their eyes, and they were

now wandering away, shaking their heads as if they were dazed. The others crowded around, congratulating Whisper.

"Come on, Golden Briar!" cried Valentina. "We need to free my aunt!"

As Golden Briar cantered toward the cave, Matilda squealed, "Isla, you and Buttercup have bonded!"

Buttercup nuzzled Isla's head. "She's right. You've got a streak of pink, yellow, and green in your hair. The same colors as my mane!"

Isla felt like she was going to explode with happiness as she and Buttercup hugged. "I still don't understand how you got here to the lagoon," she said.

"We guessed Ms. Willow had taken you here," said Matilda.

"Buttercup and Crystal worked together,

combining Buttercup's finding magic with Crystal's snow magic and making the coolest snow twister ever!" said Rosa. "We weren't sure if it was going to work, but the twister was like a huge tornado. It followed Buttercup's magical arrow and brought us to these woods."

"We didn't know where we were, but then you suddenly appeared with Valentina, Golden Briar, and Prancer!" said Ariana. "So what happened to you?"

Isla and Prancer quickly explained.

"I'm free now. I don't have to do what Ms. Willow says anymore," said Prancer happily.

"Hey, everyone!" Valentina called from the cave entrance. "My aunt and Thyme are inside, but I can't wake them up."

"They're under a spell," said Prancer. "If we take them back to the academy, one of the

teachers should know enough about spells to work with me to lift the enchantment."

"Let's go!" said Rosa.

"NO!" screamed a voice. There was a flash of light, and a bolt of magic came shooting toward them. The unicorns leaped out of the way just in time.

"I never should have trusted you!" Ms. Willow hissed at Valentina.

"Move, Golden Briar!" Valentina screamed as Ms. Willow threw a firebolt at them.

"I've got this!" Golden Briar slammed his hooves on the ground, and calling up his wind magic, he swept the firebolt to one side. It hit a tree and exploded with a terrifying bang. Flames and sparks shot into the air. Isla clutched at Buttercup's mane as they were blown sideways, crashing into Pearl. Another firebolt spun from

Ms. Willow's hand. Golden Briar forced that one away too. The trees swayed, their branches creaking and groaning in the wind.

"Everyone, over here," cried Violet. "Let Twinkle protect you."

Twinkle had created a shimmering dome of starlight. It rose over him like a curved shield. Buttercup ducked behind it, along with the other unicorns and their riders.

CRACK! CRASH! BANG!

The firebolts came fast and furious, hitting the shield and pinging off in all directions. Nearby bushes and trees burst into flames. Ms. Willow's face scrunched up, and she flung her hands to the sky. A black bolt of lightning came down and slammed into the shield. It buckled and bent.

Twinkle half closed his eyes as he tried desperately to keep the shield in place.

"Keep going, Twinkle," urged Violet, stroking his neck.

"I can't hold it for much longer." Twinkle was gasping with the effort. "We need a new plan."

Ms. Willow cackled, and an arrow of dark magic whizzed toward them, black smoke trailing behind it. It speared the dome at its center. There was a loud pop, and the shield collapsed.

"It's over!" Ms. Willow said, sneering. "Bind them!" She pointed at the unicorns.

Silver ribbons slithered out of her pockets like evil snakes. They raced across the ground toward the unicorns.

"Stay away from the binding ribbons!" cried Prancer anxiously. "If they wrap around you, you'll be under Ms. Willow's control!"

"Use your magic, Golden Briar!" cried Valentina.

Golden Briar stamped his hooves. A wind swept the ribbons straight into the branches of a tree.

Ms. Willow snarled in fury and hurled another ball of magic at Golden Briar.

BANG! As the magic exploded, Golden Briar stumbled backward, the wind dropped, and the ribbons fell to the ground. They began to slither toward the unicorns again.

Valentina threw her arms around Golden Briar's neck. "Try again! You can do it, Golden Briar. Trust me, you're amazing."

Golden Briar arched his neck proudly and banged his hooves down. The wind tore through the trees and swept the ribbons back—straight toward Ms. Willow.

"No!" she said, gasping and attempting to hurl another spell at Golden Briar, but it was too late.

The ribbons were already winding around her.
They surged over her, rapidly circling around her
until she was almost completely covered.

"Oh wow, Golden Briar!" squealed Valentina.
"Look what you did!"

With a roar, Pearl transformed into a polar bear
and leaped onto Ms. Willow, pinning her down to
stop her from getting away.

"What should we do with her?" Matilda yelled.

"I'll use my spell-weaver magic to move her to Unicorn Academy," whinnied Prancer. "The teachers can help me from there. With Ms. Willow as a prisoner, the island will be safe again. After that, I will find my real owner, Lacey. I've missed her so much. Thank you for freeing me!" She tossed her magnificent mane back and trotted over and touched her face to Ms. Willow's head. There was a flash, and the two of them vanished.

"We did it!" said Ariana, looking stunned. "We caught Ms. Willow. The island is safe again!"

Golden Briar nuzzled Valentina's neck. "I hope Prancer finds her real owner. It must be awful for them both to have been separated," he said. "I can't imagine not being with you, Valentina."

"It would be the worst feeling in the world," agreed Valentina, hugging him.

"Valentina, you've bonded! There's a golden

streak in your hair!" cried Isla, pointing. Valentina grabbed a strand of her long brown hair, and seeing the golden streak, she burst into happy tears. "Now we can graduate!" she cried.

"We're all going to graduate together!" cried Rosa. "Hip, hip, hooray!" she whooped. The others joined in, and the dark trees rang with the sound of their cheers.

CHAPTER 11

As the cheers faded, Violet was struck by a worrying thought. "How are we going to get back to the academy?"

"I can try conjuring a twister again," said Crystal eagerly. She stamped a hoof.

A few pink sparks flew up into the air, turning into pink snowflakes. They swirled together in a tornado. "It's too small," said Crystal sadly. "Making such a huge twister before must have worn my magic out."

"Don't worry," Rosa comforted her unicorn.

89

"You did great just to get us here. We'll find another way to get home."

They all exchanged looks. No one wanted to be the one to say it, but how were they going to do that?

"Girls?"

They swung around. Ms. Nettles was standing in the cave entrance, swaying slightly, her glasses sitting at a crooked angle on her nose. Her unicorn, Thyme, was standing beside her, yawning sleepily.

"What's going on?" Ms. Nettles demanded, taking her glasses off and rubbing her eyes.

"You're awake!" said

Valentina, looking relieved. "Are you all right?"

"The bad magic must be fading. Prancer said the island would be safe again now that we've captured Ms. Willow!" Isla said.

Ms. Nettles blinked. "The last thing I remember is heading off to a meeting about Ms. Willow. How did I get here?"

The girls quickly told her what had happened.

As they talked, Ms. Nettles's eyes grew wider and wider. "You really freed Prancer and captured Ms. Willow?"

"Yes," said Valentina. She smiled at her aunt. "I'm so glad you're okay. When Ms. Willow told me she'd kidnapped you, I was really worried."

"You have a good heart, Valentina," said Ms. Nettles, smiling back. "Even if it has been buried under attitude at times. But I've always had faith in you, and"—her smile got wider as her eyes

fell on the golden streak in Valentina's hair—"it appears I was right. You have finally bonded with Golden Briar."

Valentina beamed. "Isla and Buttercup have bonded too. We can all graduate—as long as we can get back to the academy in time."

"Can you help us?" Ariana asked Ms. Nettles anxiously.

"Thyme does not have transporting powers," said Ms. Nettles. "However, I have an idea. You say the Frozen Lagoon is on the other side of the trees? And underneath its surface there is all the magic that Ms. Willow has stolen from the island?"

They nodded.

Ms. Nettles vaulted onto Thyme. "Then maybe the island magic can help us. Come with me—there's no time to waste!"

They followed Ms. Nettles through the trees.

"If I'm right, then by working as a team we can

92

return to the academy *and* release the magic back to where it belongs," Ms. Nettles explained over her shoulder.

Isla felt her stomach twist with excitement. What were they going to do?

They reached the Frozen Lagoon and followed Ms. Nettles onto the thick ice. Underneath the surface, the rainbow magic bubbled as if it was desperate to be free. The unicorns slipped and slid, but they kept on going until they reached the very center of the lagoon.

"Stand in a circle, everyone. Now hold hands," said Ms. Nettles. "If we all unite, I believe we can direct our unicorns' magic into something different from their usual powers. Unicorns, you must touch each other too, and everyone must focus on melting the ice."

"Melting the ice?" said Valentina. "But won't we drown?"

"Trust the island to look after us," said Ms. Nettles confidently. "Amazing magical feats can be achieved through love and faith. With your love of each other"—her look took in all the girls and their unicorns—"and your love of the island, we can do this. Are you ready?"

Everyone nodded.

"Then form a circle. Unicorns, call up your magic and focus on what you want it to do!"

The unicorns stood shoulder to shoulder, their muzzles touching as they drummed their hooves on the ice.

Melt the ice, melt the ice, thought Isla, concentrating hard. To her surprise, sparks flew up from the unicorns' hooves and joined together above their heads in a ball of glittering light.

"Keep going, everyone!" urged Ms. Nettles.

Isla's mind filled with pictures of the ice melting. She felt Buttercup trembling.

A bright pink star suddenly shot from the glittering ball, then another and another, until suddenly there was a great fountain of stars shooting into the sky. They whizzed through the air and landed on the ice.

CRACK! CRACK! CRACK!

As the stars fell, a spiderweb spread across the icy surface and the magic water began to bubble up from underneath. The only solid ice was the circle the unicorns were standing on. More stars shot out as the icy lagoon split into pieces and melted away. The water rushed faster, swirling around the girls and unicorns on their island of ice, rising higher but not touching them. Suddenly, it exploded over the banks of the lagoon, flowing away in rainbow streams. The water was returning the magic to where it belonged.

"We've done it!" cried Ms. Nettles. "Now, Crystal, try using your magic to make a twister again. I am sure the island will help us."

Crystal slammed her hooves down on the ice, and an enormous twister of pink snowflakes whooshed around them. "It's working!" she

whinnied as the twister suddenly swept them all away.

There was a lot of explaining to do when they got back to the academy. The other teachers were delighted and very relieved to see the girls, unicorns, and Ms. Nettles back safe and sound, and to catch up on what happened. The girls heard that Ms. Willow had been bound by magic and taken away to prison. She would never be able to cast spells again.

The next day, when the girls woke up, everything seemed to glimmer and shine more brightly than ever before, as if the beautiful island was rejoicing at having its magic back. The morning was spent grooming, bathing their unicorns, and packing their bags, and after lunch, everyone's parents started to arrive for

graduation. They toured the school and stables, admiring the decorations and Matilda's mural, before it was time for each dorm to do a riding display.

Isla's heart stuttered inside her chest as she waited at the edge of the arena on Buttercup. The unicorns' coats shone, and the sparkly ribbons braided through their manes and tails looked beautiful. Ruby dorm was first, and the parents clapped loudly as Buttercup found various things hidden around the arena, and then Golden Briar transported back to Valentina with his wind magic. Anna's unicorn, Lumiere, created an amazing light display while Molly's unicorn, Sparkle, played some music.

Next, it was Diamond dorm's turn. Isla clapped as Honey thrilled everyone with her super-speed, Pearl used a glamour to turn into a snarling tiger,

and Whisper soothed her with calming magic. Then Crystal carried everyone to the center of the arena in a snow twister, where Twinkle covered them with a glittering shield.

The riding displays were followed by the actual graduation ceremony. As night fell, students and unicorns filed into the ballroom to huge applause from the parents and teachers.

"Stay back, give us some space so my parents can see me," Valentina said as Buttercup trotted up behind Golden Briar.

Isla grinned. "That's the bossy Valentina we know and love," she whispered to Buttercup. Valentina had softened up a lot over the year, but it was clear that her snooty side hadn't left her. Isla didn't mind. Valentina had more than proved that her heart was in the right place.

As Ms. Nettles started her speech, Isla looked around at her friends and thought how much she was going to miss them. They would definitely keep in touch, though. Violet had already arranged a sleepover at her house. Ms. Nettles's voice broke into Isla's thoughts.

"Graduating students and unicorns, the staff and I are very proud of your achievements. You came here as strangers and leave as lifelong friends. Wherever you go on the island, know that your friends are with you." Ms. Nettles paused as everyone cheered and clapped. "And now," she said, as silence fell again, "please come and collect your scrolls."

Isla was so happy to receive her graduation scroll that, when she'd shaken hands with Ms. Nettles and Ms. Rosemary, she turned to wave it at her own and Buttercup's parents.

"Party time!" said Buttercup as they got off the stage.

The ballroom was hung with snowflakes, and the long tables were piled high with so much delicious food—tiny sandwiches, chocolate cakes, plates of unicorn-shaped cookies, fruit platters, and a huge unicorn made out of sugar. Some of the students and unicorns danced while others talked or gathered around the table, eating and drinking.

Isla and Diamond dorm took plates of treats outside to the banks of the lake. The rainbow-colored water shone in the moonlight, and behind the lake, the marble school buildings stood against the star-studded sky.

"It's so beautiful," said Rosa. "I'm glad we managed to stop Ms. Willow. Just imagine if she'd captured all our unicorns."

"It would have been awful," Ariana said softly.

Violet smiled at Isla. "I'm so happy we graduated together."

Isla nodded, her hands playing in Buttercup's long silky mane. "And Valentina too." She looked over to where Valentina was dancing with Golden Briar.

"Yes," said Matilda. "She's changed a lot this year."

"We all have," said Violet thoughtfully. "But isn't that part of being at Unicorn Academy? To learn about our unicorns and ourselves?"

"I'm going to miss it," said Isla softly. "And all of you."

"Don't get sad now," said Matilda quickly. "There's Violet's sleepover to look forward to, remember?"

"And we're going to go on vacation together every summer!" said Freya.

They all smiled.

"Just think how good our magic will be by next summer after we've practiced some more!" said Buttercup.

Isla hugged her. "Your magic is really good already. I'm sorry I ever doubted you. When you asked it to find Ms. Willow and it took us to Ms. Nettles in the shed, you were right. It was Ms. Willow in disguise!"

"Everyone's magic has been useful," said Rosa. "We worked as a team."

"Because that's when unicorns and their riders are strongest," said Buttercup, looking at Isla through her eyelashes.

Violet smiled at Twinkle. "You know, I think that might be the most important lesson of all." There was a whizzing noise and a bang, and the sky was suddenly filled with pink and purple stars.

"Fireworks!" Rosa gasped.

More and more fireworks shot into the air and

filled the sky until a final one formed the figure of a unicorn.

Everyone clapped and cheered once more. Isla wrapped her arms around Buttercup's neck, her heart swelling as she watched the unicorn shining high above them. She'd bonded with Buttercup, she'd just graduated, and she'd had the best year of her life.

"I'm so glad you're my unicorn," she told Buttercup. "From now on, I'm definitely going to be more like you. I'll believe in myself and be braver, and I'm going to speak out instead of worrying that people might think I'm silly."

Buttercup blew on her hair. "Well, I'm going to try to be more like *you* and think more before I jump in. Maybe attacking an enchanted wolf on my own wasn't the smartest thing to do!"

Isla giggled and buried her face in Buttercup's mane, breathing in her sweet unicorn smell.

"We'll work together to protect Unicorn Island," she promised.

"And each other," said Buttercup, her dark eyes shining with love.

"Always," said Isla with a smile.

What if you could save Unicorn Island? Don't miss Unicorn Academy Nature Magic, a brand-new magical series about the environment!

Strange purple tornadoes are hitting villages around Unicorn Academy! Can Lily and Feather stop them *and* save the school?

Read on for a peek at the first book in the Unicorn Academy Nature Magic series!

"Here we are, Lils," Lily's mom said. "Unicorn Academy—your home for the next year!"

"Oh, wow!" Lily's breath rushed out as she stared up at the enormous glass-and-marble building. On the top of the tallest tower, a pink flag with a white unicorn on it was rippling in the breeze. "It's beautiful," she said. She looked at the gardens full of winter plants and flowers, and the lake shimmering in the distance.

Her mother smiled. "It is, isn't it? It hasn't changed one bit since I was here. You're going to have such a fantastic time. I just know it!"

Lily couldn't speak. Her stomach felt like it was tying itself in knots. She'd wanted to come to Unicorn Academy for ages—she couldn't wait to be paired with a unicorn and start training to become a guardian of beautiful Unicorn Island. However, now that she was here and the academy looked so big, she was beginning to wonder whether her invitation to become a student had been a mistake. The other new students all looked so confident as they chatted with each other and waved goodbye to their parents.

What if I'm not good enough to be a guardian? Lily thought with a rush of panic. *What if I mess things up and get asked to leave? Mom will be so disappointed.*

A teacher walked up. She wore her brown hair in a neat bun held in place with silver clips. Three girls were following her.

"Hello, I'm Ms. Rosemary. I teach Care of Unicorns. And what's your name?" the teacher said to Lily.

Lily was feeling so overwhelmed, the words seemed to stick in her throat. "I'm . . . um . . . um . . . ," she stammered.

"Lily Jamieson," her mom offered.

Ms. Rosemary looked at her clipboard. "That's lucky! Lily, you're going to be in Amethyst dorm with these three. This is Aisha." She pointed to a girl who was carrying a flute case and had curly black hair in a high ponytail. The girl grinned at Lily, who smiled shyly back.

"And this is Zara," Ms. Rosemary continued. Zara had dark brown hair that stopped just past her shoulders and green eyes. She studied Lily for a moment and then gave her a smile.

"And Phoebe," Ms. Rosemary finished. Phoebe

was tall and slim, with honey-blond hair in two waist-length braids. She grinned.

"Hi, Lily! Isn't this super awesome!" She swept her arms out. "I mean, look around. It's gorgeous, isn't it? We're just so lucky to have been invited to be students here!"

Lily thought it sounded like everything Phoebe said had an exclamation mark after it.

"Say goodbye to your mom, Lily," said Ms. Rosemary. "Then we need to get to the hall. It's almost time for the ceremony where you will be paired with your unicorns."

Lily felt a flutter of delight. She was going to have a unicorn of her own!

MERMICORNs

Swim into a new series!

MERMICORNs 1

Sparkle Magic

Sudipta Bardhan-Quallen

Mermicorns are part unicorn, part mermaid, and totally magical!

Meet your newest feline friends!

PURRMAIDS

The Scaredy Cat

Sudipta Bardhan-Quallen

New friends. New adventures.
Find a new series ... just for you!

ISADORA MOON

ISADORA MOON
Goes to School

Harriet Muncaster

For ballerina and fairy and vampire lovers

MAGIC ON THE MAP

MAGIC ON THE MAP
LET'S MOOOVE!

COURTNEY SHEINMEL & BIANCA TURETSKY

For adventurers

UNICORN ACADEMY

UNICORN ACADEMY
Sophia and Rainbow

JULIE SYKES illustrated by LUCY TRUMAN

For unicorn lovers

PUPPY PIRATES

PUPPY PIRATES
Stowaway!

Erin Soderberg

For dog lovers

PuRRmaids

PuRRmaids
The Scaredy Cat

For mermaid and cat lovers

BALLPARK Mysteries

BALLPARK Mysteries
THE WORLD SERIES CURSE

David A. Kelly

For sports fans

Collect all the books in the Horse Diaries series!

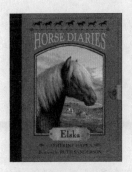

HORSE DIARIES

Elska

CATHERINE HAPKA
Illustrated by RUTH SANDERSON

HORSE DIARIES

Bell's Star

ALISON HART
Illustrated by RUTH SANDERSON

HORSE DIARIES

Koda

PATRICIA HERMES
Illustrated by RUTH SANDERSON

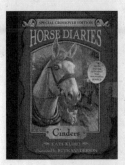

HORSE DIARIES

Luna

CATHERINE HAPKA
Illustrated by RUTH SANDERSON

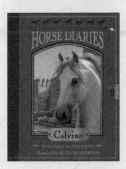

SPECIAL CROSSOVER EDITION

HORSE DIARIES

Cinders

KATE KLIMO
Illustrated by RUTH SANDERSON

HORSE DIARIES

Calvino

WHITNEY SANDERSON
Illustrated by RUTH SANDERSON